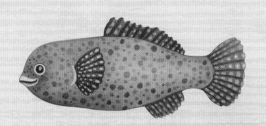

ALL ABOUT
MERMAIDS

FOR JINX, WHOSE IDEA IT WAS TO WRITE
A NONFICTION BOOK ABOUT MERMAIDS
—IZZY

FOR MY LIFE PARTNER, DANICA JOVANOVIC, FOR ALL
YOUR ENCOURAGEMENT AND INVALUABLE SUPPORT,
AND FOR INSPIRING ME TO PURSUE MY DREAMS
—VLAD

Text copyright © 2019 by Izzy Quinn
Jacket and interior illustrations copyright © 2019 by Vlad Stankovic

All rights reserved. Published in the United States by Crown Books for Young Readers,
an imprint of Random House Children's Books, a division of Penguin Random House LLC, New York.
Originally published in Australia in slightly different form by Little Hare Books, an imprint of
Hardie Grant Egmont, Richmond, Victoria, in 2019.

Crown and the colophon are registered trademarks of Penguin Random House LLC.

Visit us on the Web! rhcbooks.com

Educators and librarians, for a variety of teaching tools, visit us at
RHTeachersLibrarians.com

Library of Congress Cataloging-in-Publication Data
Names: Quinn, Izzy, author. | Stankovic, Vlad, illustrator.
Title: All about mermaids / written by Izzy Quinn ; illustrated by Vlad Stankovic.
Description: First edition. | New York : Crown Books for Young Readers, 2021. |
Audience: Ages 3–7 | Summary: "Dive into the world of mermaids and discover everything there is to know
about the ocean's most mysterious creatures, from where they are found and how they sleep, to what they
eat and how they raise their young. Overflowing with fascinating facts and spellbinding artwork, *All About
Mermaids* is the ultimate book for young mermaid enthusiasts" —Provided by publisher.
Identifiers: LCCN 2020032243 (print) | LCCN 2020032244 (ebook) |
ISBN 978-0-593-30715-1 (hardcover) | ISBN 978-0-593-30716-8 (library binding) |
ISBN 978-0-593-30717-5 (ebook)
Subjects: LCSH: Mermaids—Juvenile literature.
Classification: LCC GR910 .Q56 2021 (print) | LCC GR910 (ebook) |
DDC 398.21—dc23

The text of this book is set in 14-point Baskerville.
The illustrations in this book were created using watercolors, colored pencils, and Photoshop.

MANUFACTURED IN CHINA
10 9 8 7 6 5 4 3 2 1
First American Edition

WRITTEN BY IZZY QUINN   ILLUSTRATED BY VLAD STANKOVIC

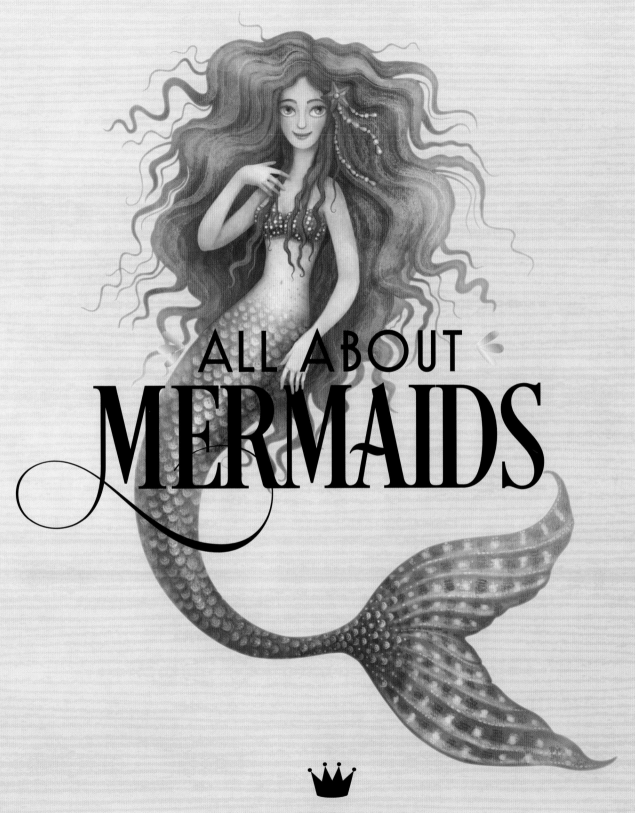

ALL ABOUT
MERMAIDS

Crown Books for Young Readers
New York

Tales from every corner of the world tell of mermaids enchanting unwary sailors with their beautiful song, calling up storms, and causing shipwrecks— but these stories are the result of superstition and misunderstanding. Mermaids are our closest relatives, and they live and eat and sleep and play and raise their young together, just like we do. You might be surprised as you read this book to find out how similar we are.

Some people say that mermaids are a figment of our imaginations—that long-ago sailors saw dugongs or Steller's sea cows through their spyglasses and mistook them for women combing their hair and singing. That is complete nonsense, as anyone who has ever seen or heard a dugong can tell you. The only thing less like a mermaid you could imagine is a huffing, sighing, snorting sea cow—a majestic, slow-moving beast the size of a small whale, now sadly extinct.

Mermaid

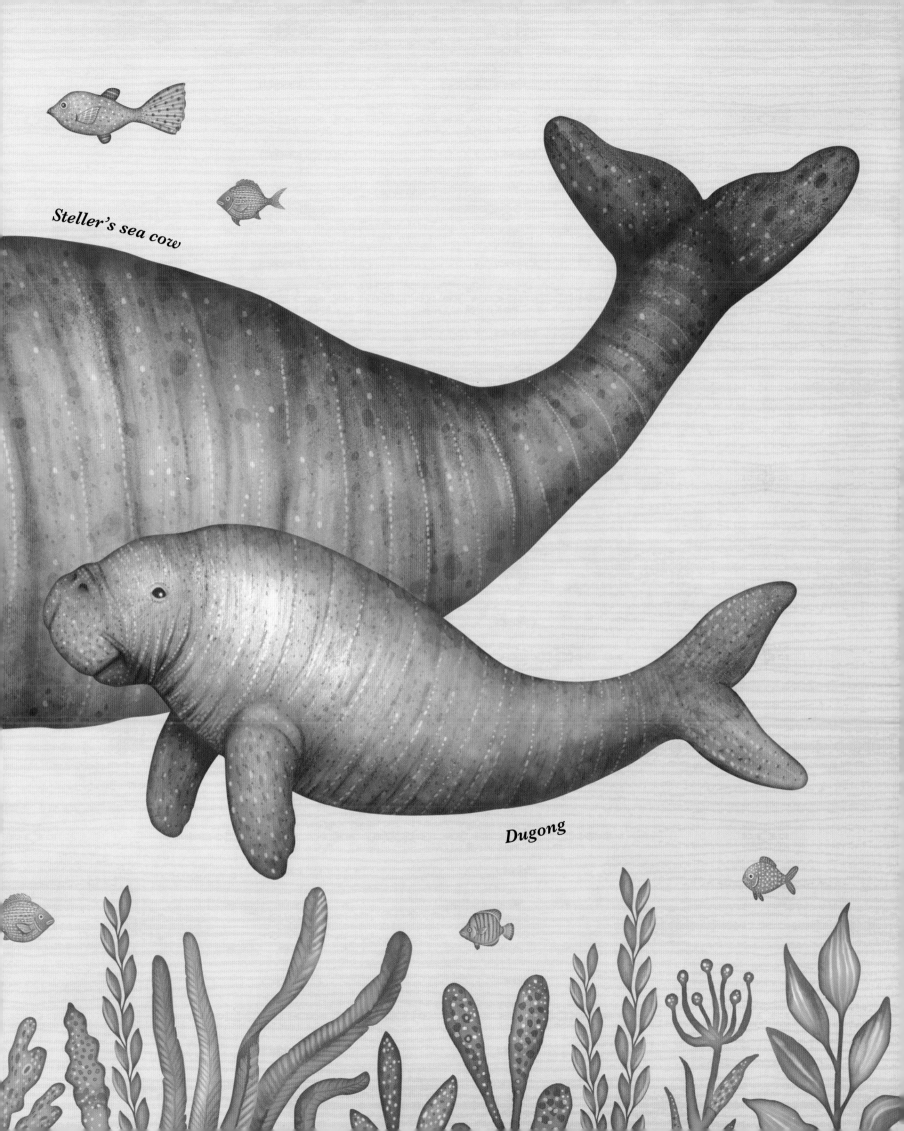

Steller's sea cow

Dugong

Mermaids are built for speed, streaking through the water far more swiftly than a dugong ever could. Everyone knows that mermaids have powerful tails, but did you know that they have webbing between their fingers too? Their hands look a little like a duck's feet, or maybe a frog's.

Webbed fingers

Luxuriant locks

Swishing fins

Muscular tail

In storybooks, mermaids have glittering scales, like a fish. In real life, they have smooth, sleek tails. The lacy patterns on a mermaid's tail often look like scales, though, especially when seen underwater. These markings help a mermaid to blend into her surroundings.

For the same reason, mermaids' tails are usually silver, gray, green, or blue. Vivid, jewel-like reds, pinks, purples, and oranges are seen only in warmer waters, where tropical fish dart about against a background of brightly colored corals.

When they swim, mermaids move their tails up and down— not from side to side, as fish do.

Like dolphins, whales, and dugongs, most mermaids have tails that end in horizontal flukes. Forked twin tails were once common but are now extremely rare.

Mermaids' hair is usually black, brown, red, yellow, or green, like seaweed. Some have fine, straight, silky hair that billows around them in the water like a cloud. Others have springy, spiraling tendrils or thick, rope-like locks.

Mermaids love to groom one another and spend hours every day twisting, teasing, and braiding each other's hair as they bask in the sun.

Elaborate hairstyles are worn to celebrate special occasions. It is a point of pride among mermaids to invent new and more intricate styles.

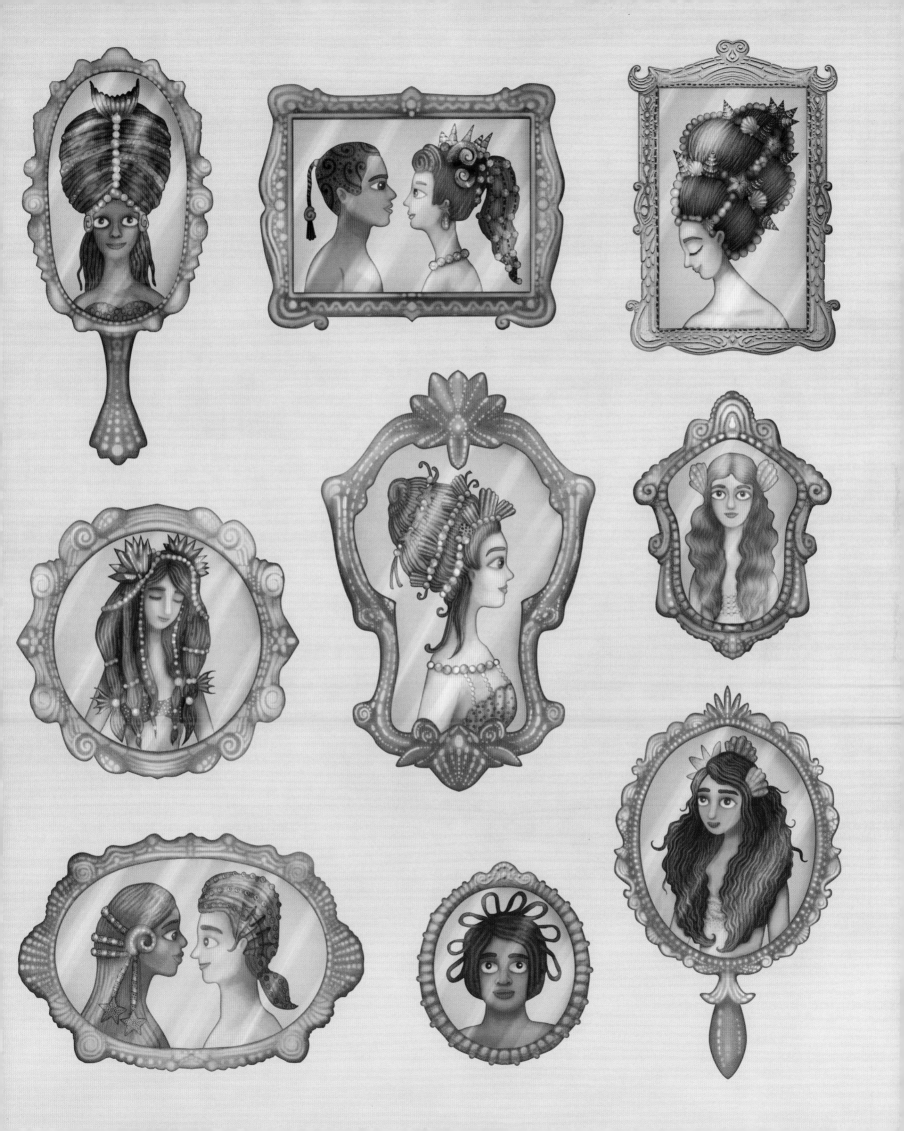

Mermaids are found everywhere in the world, in all but the coldest, wildest, most dangerous waters. Some like to stay close to shore, while others prefer the vast open ocean.

Like humans, mermaids come in all shapes and sizes—big and small, long and short. Their skin can be pale, dark, or any shade in between. What they all have in common is a love of music—and of shiny, glittery things!

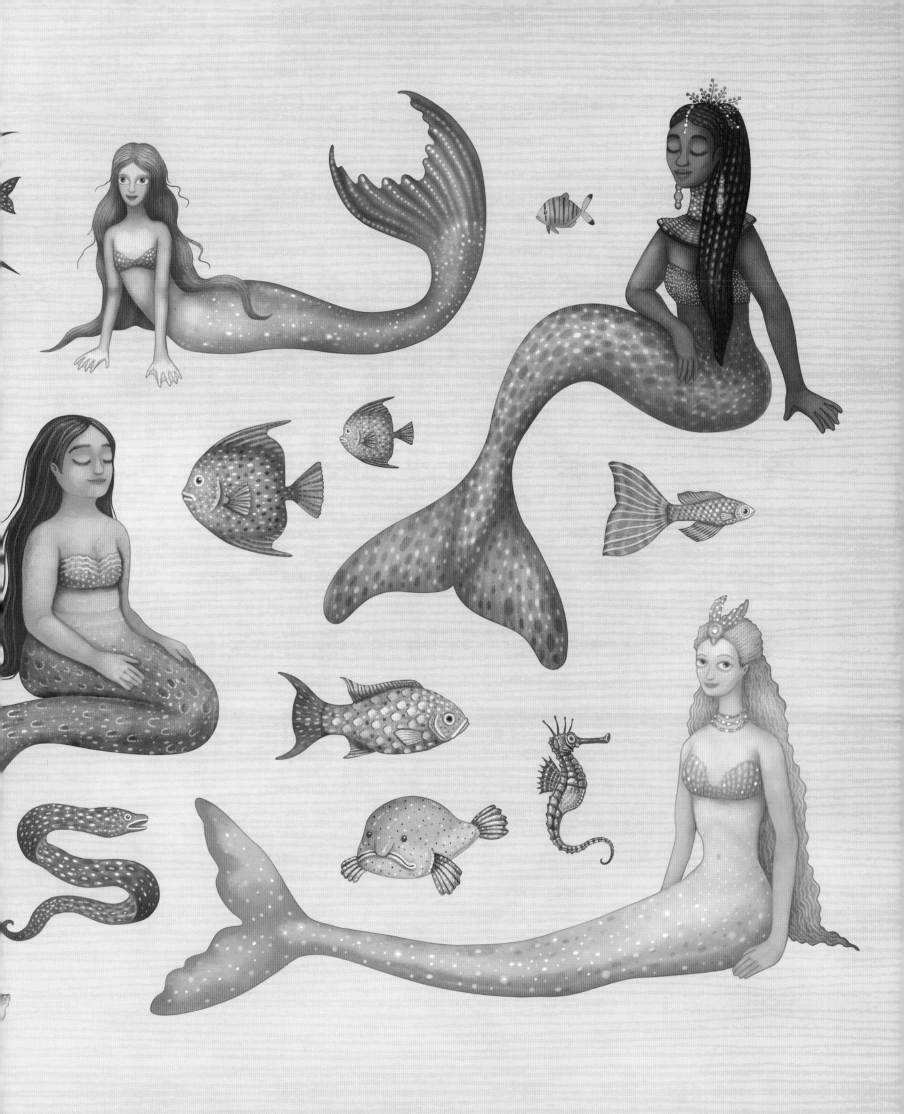

Storybooks and films often show mermaids living in ornate palaces under the sea. In fact, they spend most of their time near the surface, in the sunlight, where the water is warm, and dive only to hunt for food.

"Mermaid" means "woman of the sea," but mermaids also make their homes in rivers and lakes. Freshwater mermaids were once an everyday sight, even in big, bustling port towns. They can still be found in the world's wild places, living in high mountain streams or remote water holes in the desert, but sightings are now few and far between.

Mermaids are famous for the hypnotic beauty of their song. Humans find it spellbinding—though we cannot understand it any more than we can fathom birdsong, or the strange, haunting symphonies of the whales.

Mermaids usually live in family groups called pods. Males leave the pod at around ten or eleven years of age to find their own territory.

Mermen are solitary creatures and often prefer to live alone. Despite their fierce reputation, they are actually rather shy.

With no one to scrape the barnacles from their backs or groom their beards, adult males appear shaggy and unkempt, and have occasionally been mistaken for sea monsters.

Newborn mermaids are called whelps. They are born knowing how to swim. As the babies grow older, one of their favorite games is to hide from one another, peek out, and then, if they are seen, swim away as fast as they can. They are having fun, but they are learning too. Stealth and speed will help them to track prey—and escape from predators—when they are fully grown.

Mermaids have healthy appetites. They graze on algae and other edible plants, scour riverbanks for turtle eggs, snails, and other such delicacies, and set traps along the coast for curious crustaceans. Those who live in the open ocean are skilled hunters and survive on a diet of fish.

With their clever, nimble fingers, mermaids are good at making things: from lobster pots and fishing nets to hooks, horns, harps, and hairpins.

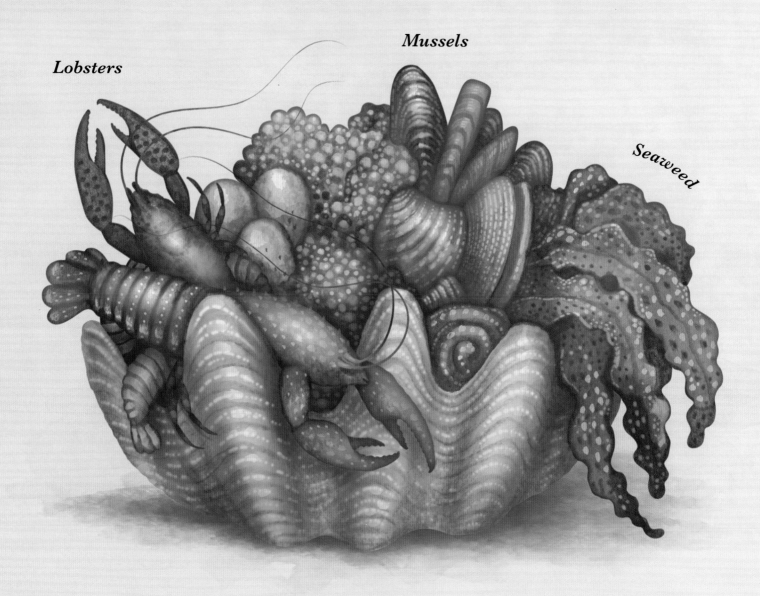

Lobsters

Mussels

Seaweed

If you look carefully as you stroll along the sand, you might, if you're very lucky, find a delicate comb carved from shell, or even a mermaid's purse.

Mermaid mirrors are famous throughout the world and sought after by collectors.

When they aren't doing each other's hair, hunting for food, or busy making things, mermaids like to nap.

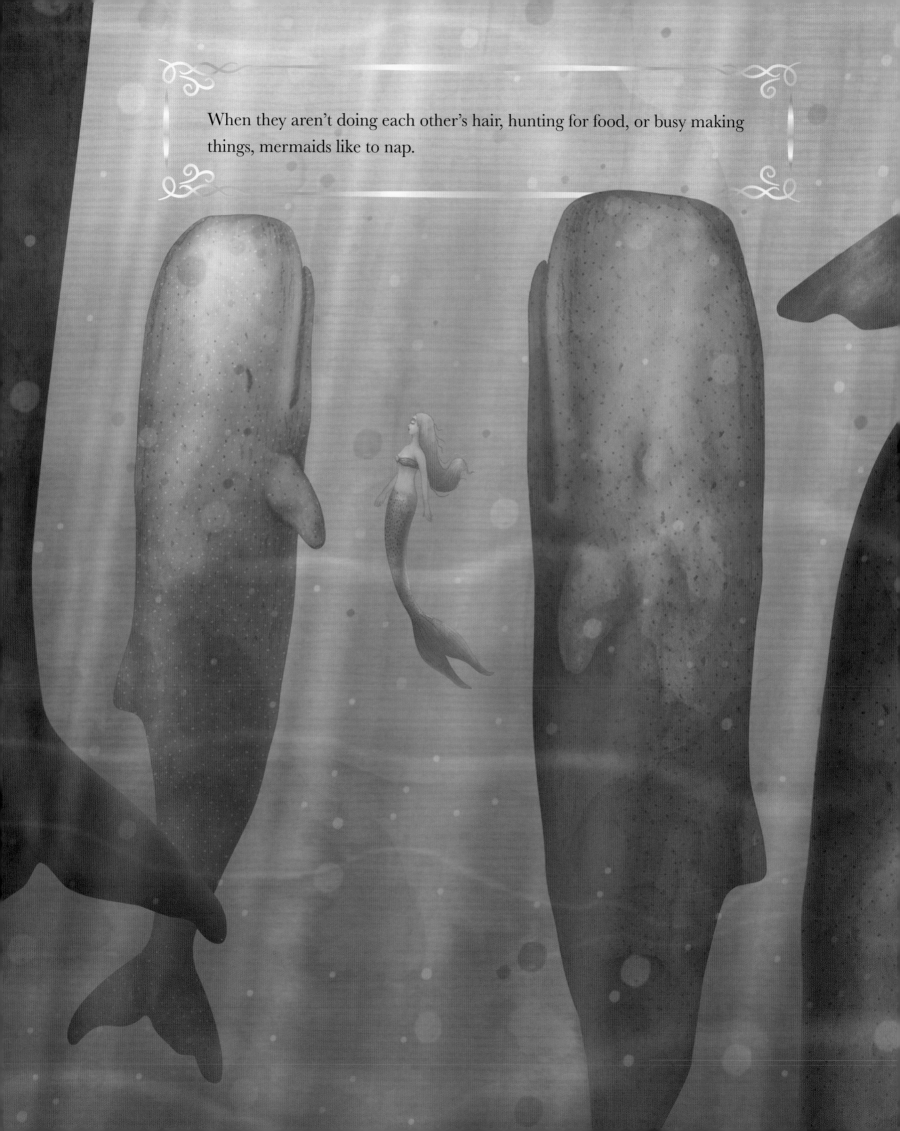

Every now and then you might spot one dozing on rocks in the sun. Most prefer to sleep in the open ocean, floating upright—often in the company of sperm whales, who like to sleep that way too.

Mermaids are sometimes heard singing just before a storm blows in. Sailors once believed they sang to summon the waves, but they are more likely warning others that wild weather is on the way.

If you see a mermaid leap from the water by moonlight, twirling and spinning through the air, there are calm waters and clear skies ahead.

Mermaids are great friends of dolphins, with whom they swim and hunt.

Whelps, like all infants, love to play with other babies and are often seen frolicking with seal pups.

The only species mermaids fear are great white sharks and orcas—and, of course, humans.

Orca

Great white shark

Human

Even today, some people refuse to believe in mermaids. It's true we rarely see them, but it's not because they don't exist. They're just shy and give humans a wide berth. Wherever there are dolphins, though, there's a good chance mermaids are nearby.

If you go down to the water and wait, sooner or later you'll see one. Be as still and quiet as you can—no splashing or shouting. If she smiles at you, smile back. Try a small wave. It will take time—but once you win a mermaid's trust, you'll have a friend forever.

Many thanks and lots of love to Abbey, Celi, Piper, Jinx, and Ginger, for sharing with me everything they know about mermaids; Bailey, for telling me all about whales and sharks; Mum, for teaching me to read; and Dad, for taking us all out on the boat.

A huge thank-you also to my publishers, for their belief in mermaids and in this book—especially my editor at Hardie Grant, Alyson O'Brien, and designer Pooja Desai. And at Crown in the US, my editor Emily Easton, copyeditor Melinda Ackell, and designer Monique Razzouk.

—Izzy

A big thank-you to Alyson O'Brien and Pooja Desai for the opportunity to be a part of this magical book, and for your patience and wonderful cooperation.

—Vlad